Little Funnies is a delightful collection of picture books made to put a giggle into storytime.

There are funny stories about a laughing lobster, a daring mouse, a teeny tiny woman, and lots more colourful characters!

Perfect for sharing, these rib-tickling tales will have your little ones coming back for more!

For Carol
P.R.

To little Sophie,
my great-niece,
with love
H.C.

First published 1996 by Walker Books Ltd
87 Vauxhall Walk, London SE11 5HJ

This edition published 2007

2 4 6 8 10 9 7 5 3 1

This book has been typeset in Calligraphic Antique.

Printed in China

British Library Cataloguing in Publication Data:
a catalogue record for this book is available from the British Library.

ISBN 978-1-4063-0785-6

www.walkerbooks.co.uk

ONE WINDY WEDNESDAY

Written by

Phyllis Root

Illustrated by

Helen Craig

WALKER BOOKS
AND SUBSIDIARIES
LONDON • BOSTON • SYDNEY • AUCKLAND

One Wednesday, Bonnie Bumble felt the wind begin to blow.

It blew
and it blew
and it blew.

It blew the
quack right out
of the duck.

It blew the moo
right out of
the cow.

It blew the oink right out of the pig.

It blew the baa right out of the lamb.

"Moo!" said the duck.

"Oink!" said the cow.
OINK!

"Quack!" said the lamb.
QUACK!

"Baa!" said the pig.
BAA!
"What a mess!" said Bonnie Bumble.

When the wind died down
she worked to put everything right.

She patted the
quack back on
to the duck.

She hitched the moo back on to the cow.

She tied the oink back
on to the pig.

She knitted the baa
back on to the lamb.

"Moo!"
said the cow.

"Quack!"
said the duck.

"Oink!"
said the pig.

"Baa!"
said the lamb.

"That's better," said
Bonnie Bumble,
all worn out.

Just then a little breeze blew by.
"Meow, meow, meow,"
said the dog!

MEOW!

Little Funnies
Joke Time
What do you call a cat with eight legs that likes to swim?
An octopuss!